Universal Edition

easy BLUE trumpet

for trumpet and piano

Rob Hudson

www.universaledition.com

vienna · london · new york

UE 21 263

ISMN M-008-07550-6
UPC 8-03452-02282-4
ISBN 3-7024-2741-4

Preface

Easy Blue Trumpet is a collection of ten original pieces written to provide an introduction to various blues styles. Most are variations on the standard twelve-measure (bar) blues song form, sometimes with a contrasting middle section. The exceptions, *Hymn* and *Lament*, are lyrical etudes with blues-type melodic shapes.

Chord symbols are included in the piano parts to aid improvisation. Accompanists may use the chord symbols to elaborate on the written piano part. For more advanced trumpet players, each piece could be repeated in a melody – improvised solo – melody format.

Capped accents, in the jazz style, are interpreted differently from those encountered in classical music. They imply not only a strong, accented articulation, as in classical styles, but also some detachment from the following note. Brass players can treat this marking similarly to staccato articulation, but with a sharper accent leaving a slightly "fatter" sounding note than staccato. If staccato articulation were represented by the syllable "dit", the capped accent can be best produced with the syllable "daht", with articulation at the end of the note as well as the beginning.

April 2004   Rob Hudson

Vorwort

Easy Blue Trumpet ist eine Sammlung von zehn speziell für diese Ausgabe komponierten Stücken zur Einführung in verschiedene Blues-Stile. Die meisten sind Variationen über die übliche zwölftaktige Bluesform, manchmal mit einem kontrastierenden Mittelteil. Als lyrische Etüden mit bluesartiger Melodieführung bilden *Hymn* und *Lament* die Ausnahme.

Der Klavierstimme wurden Akkordsymbole hinzugefügt, um das Improvisieren zu fördern. Klavier-begleiter können die Akkordsymbole nutzen, um den gedruckten Klaviersatz auszuschmücken. Fortgeschrittene Trompeter können jedes Stück in der Reihenfolge Melodie – improvisiertes Solo – Melodie wiederholen.

Akzentzeichen werden im Jazz anders als in der klassischen Musik interpretiert. Sie bedeuten nicht nur eine starke Betonung wie im klassischen Stil, sondern auch eine gewisse Trennung von der darauf folgenden Note. Blechbläser können diese Vortragsanweisung ähnlich wie ein Staccato behandeln, allerdings mit einem schärferen Akzent, der eine etwas „fetter" klingende Note als ein reines Staccato hervorruft. Wenn man das Spielen eines Staccatos mit der Silbe „dit" kennzeichnen würde, könnte man Akzente am besten mit der Silbe „daht" bilden, wobei man sowohl den Anfang als auch das Ende der Note artikuliert.

April 2004   Rob Hudson

Préface

Easy Blue Trumpet est un recueil de dix pièces composées spécialement pour cette édition et destinées à l'initiation aux différents styles blues. La plupart sont des variations sur la forme blues habituelle de douze mesures, parfois avec une partie centrale contrastée. *Hymn* et *Lament,* en tant qu'études lyriques avec une conduite mélodique de type blues, constituent l'exception.

Des figures d'accords ont été ajoutées à la partie de piano, afin de favoriser l'improvisation. Les pianistes accompagnateurs peuvent utiliser les figures d'accords pour embellir l'écriture du piano imprimée. Les trompettistes de niveau avancé peuvent répéter chaque pièce dans la succession mélodie – solo improvisé – mélodie.

Dans le jazz, les accents sont interprétés autrement que dans la musique classique. Ils ne sont pas simplement synonymes d'une forte accentuation comme dans le style classique, mais aussi d'une séparation certaine de la note qui suit. Les cuivres peuvent traiter cette indication d'exécution de manière identique à un staccato, mais avec un accent plus fort qui provoque une note sonnant « plus grassement » qu'un pur staccato. Si l'on indiquait l'exécution d'un staccato avec la syllabe « dit », on pourrait au mieux former des accents avec la syllabe « daht » ; on doit alors articuler aussi bien le début que la fin de la note.

Avril 2004   Rob Hudson

Contents · Inhalt · Table des Matières

2

Blues for Benny

Rob Hudson

Universal Edition UE 21 263

3

4

Low Down Blues

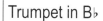

BLUE TRUMPET

easy

Rob Hudson

Blues for Benny

Universal Edition UE 21 263a

Low Down Blues

∧ = short

Funky, lazy swing feel ♩ = 100

Jump Blues

Bouncing Medium Swing ♩ = 120

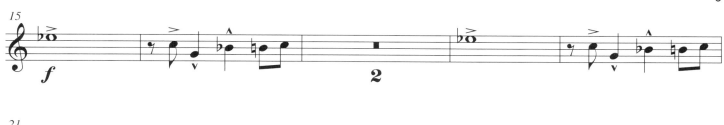

Old Time Blues

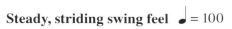

UE 21 263a

Blues for Cannonball

Down Home Blues

Lament

Blues for Mingus

Riff Blues

Hymn

Universal Edition

6

Jump Blues

Old Time Blues

Blues for Cannonball

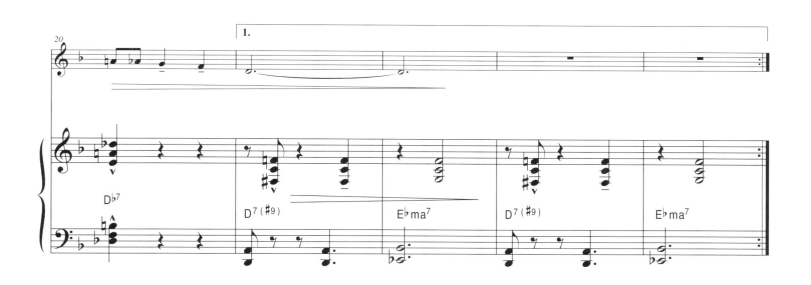

Down Home Blues

Lament

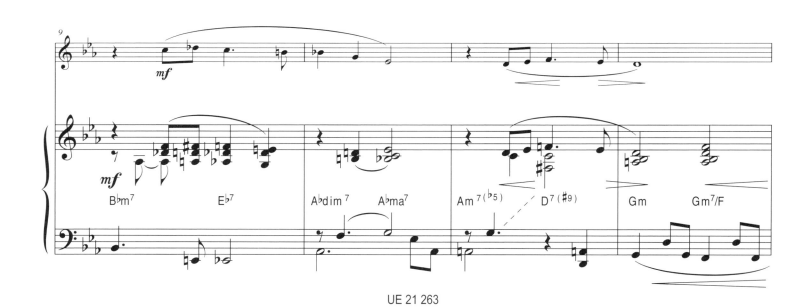

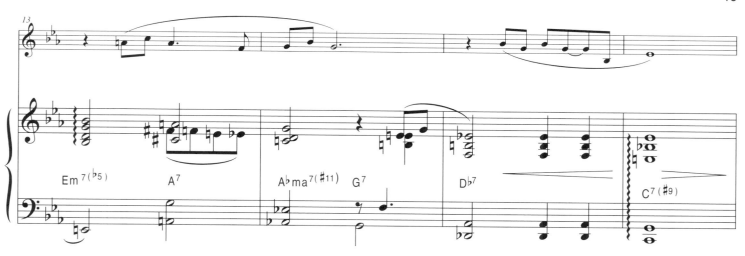

rit.   molto rit.

Blues for Mingus

Riff Blues

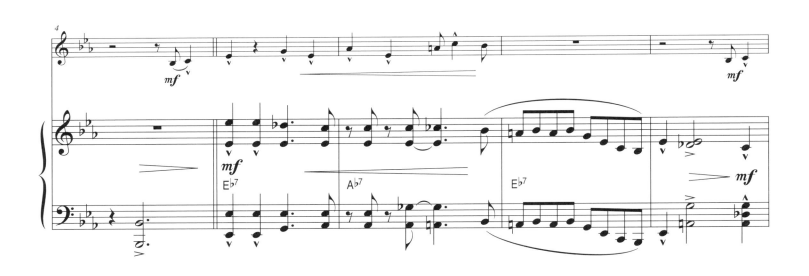

Hymn